Lucy's Lab

The Colossal Fossil Fiasco

D1016140

Lucy's Lab

The Colossal Fossil Fiasco

by Michelle Houts
Illustrated by Elizabeth Zechel

Sky Pony Press
New York

First Edition

This is a work of fiction. Names, characters, places, and incidents are from the authors' imaginations and are used fictitiously.

Sky Pony Press books may be purchased in bulk at special discounts for sales promotion, corporate gifts, fund-raising, or educational purposes. Special editions can also be created to specifications. For details, contact the Special Sales Department, Sky Pony Press, 307 West 36th Street, 11th Floor, New York, NY 10018 or info@skyhorsepublishing.com.

Sky Pony® is a registered trademark of Skyhorse Publishing, Inc.®, a Delaware corporation.

Visit our website at www.skyponypress.com.
Books, authors, and more at www.skyponypressblog.com.

www.michellehouts.com.
www.elizabethzechel.com.

10 9 8 7 6 5 4 3 2 1

Library of Congress Cataloging-in-Publication Data

Names: Houts, Michelle, author. | Zechel, Elizabeth, illustrator.
Title: The colossal fossil fiasco / Michelle Houts ; Illustrated by Elizabeth Zechel.
Description: First edition. | New York : Sky Pony Press, Skyhorse Publishing, [2018] | Series: Lucy's lab ; #3 | Summary: While her second-grade class is studying fossils, Lucy makes an important discovery but her classmate, Stewart, claims credit. |
Identifiers: LCCN 2017043705 (print) | LCCN 2017057185 (ebook) | ISBN 9781510710726 (eb) | ISBN 9781510710702 (hc : alk. paper) | ISBN 9781510710719 (pb : alk. paper) | ISBN 9781510710726 (ebook)
Subjects: | CYAC: Fossils—Fiction. | Honesty—Fiction. | Schools—Fiction. | Family life—Fiction.
Classification: LCC PZ7.H8235 (ebook) | LCC PZ7.H8235 Col 2018 (print) | DDC [E]—dc23
LC record available at https://lccn.loc.gov/2017043705

Cover illustration by Elizabeth Zechel
Cover design by Kate Gartner

Printed in Canada

Contents

Chapter One

Snow Day

"Look outside!" Thomas yells. "Hurry, Lucy!"

He's staring out of the living room window, still wearing his T. rex pajamas.

"There's no reason to hurry," Dad tells Thomas. "I don't think the snow is going away any time soon."

I walk over to the window and stand beside my little brother. My own flannel pajamas are warm and cozy, but I kind of wish they had feet like Thomas's. My bare toes are cold, even on the living room carpet.

1

Outside, the snow that fell overnight is blowing in crazy circles all around the yard. There's a drift in front of the garage door with two tire tracks through it that mom's car made when she left for work. I can't wait to get outside and play!

"Dad," I ask, "do you think we'll have—"

The kitchen phone rings. Dad's cell phone lights up at the very same moment.

He grins. "There's the robo call. Do you think we should answer?"

"Dad!" I run for the phone on the kitchen counter.

"Hello?"

"This-is-a-mes-sage-from-Gran-ite-Cit-y-Schools," the computer voice on the other end says. "The-Gran-ite-Cit-y-Schools-will-be-closed-to-day-due-to-in-clem-ent-weath-er. Thank-you."

"Thank you," I tell the robo voice, and I hang up the phone. "Yes! It's a snow day!"

Thomas turns away from the window. "Why did a robot call us? To tell us it snowed?"

Thomas is only four. There's so much about life he doesn't understand.

"There isn't really a robot, Thomas," I explain. "It's just an automatic phone call saying that I don't have to go to school today!"

"Do I have to go to school today?" Thomas asks. He's not old enough for kindergarten, but he thinks the Wee Care

Daycare Center is school. I look at Dad. I'm not sure if daycare has a robo-call system.

"Your school is up and running. It's business as usual for you, Thomas," Dad says. My brother makes a grouchy face. "And for me. I'd better get to the business of plowing, or I'll have some very unhappy customers."

Dad finishes his coffee and gathers extra gloves while Thomas goes upstairs to get dressed. Dad's a landscaper all summer. That means he plants bushes and mows grass. In the winter, he shovels sidewalks and clears the snow from parking lots. I guess that makes him a land-*scraper* all winter!

"I'll drop you at the library before I take Thomas to daycare," Dad says to me.

Thank goodness we have an arrangement with Aunt Darian. I spend snow days at the library where she works. Cousin Cora and I will help her put books back on the shelves, and we'll read in one of the study rooms, and we'll go to the Talking Room where we can laugh out loud.

"Why can't *I* go to the library?" Thomas is back, and he's wearing a winter hat that our grandma in Ohio knitted. It's green and has dinosaur spikes down the back.

Dad grins. "Because Granite City has strict rules about dinosaurs in the public library."

Chapter Two

Biographies

When I jump out of Dad's truck in front of the library, Cora is there waiting to let me in the locked door. The library doesn't actually open until 9:30, but I get special privileges, since I'm the niece of the children's librarian.

"Can you believe it?" Cora asks. "It's our first snow day of second grade!"

She's using her normal voice, which is kind of loud and excited. That's okay, since the library isn't open.

"Dad thinks the snow will all be melted

by tomorrow, since the ground isn't very cold yet," I tell her, "so we better get outside soon."

"My mom says we have to stay inside the library until after lunch. Then we can go out." Cora shrugs.

That's okay with me. I have a lot of research to do, and a whole morning in the library sounds perfect.

"Where do you want to go first?" I ask, even though I already know the answer. Cora has always been wild about the Cindy Sparkles books. I can see why, too. Cora could have been the model for the covers. Cora and Cindy both have bouncy blonde hair. They both love pink and purple and everything they wear has to glitter, at least a little.

"Biographies," Cora answers.

I think my eyes must bulge out of

my head like the eyes of a grasshopper. "Biographies? Really?"

"Yep," says Cora. "Follow me!" She twirls in her hot pink skirt and skips along in her hot pink ballet shoes toward the section where all the books have a capital *B* on the spine.

I love biographies. Sometimes they are kind of thick, but most have words I can read—or figure out—with drawings or photos inside, and amazing true stories about real people. Sometimes, the people are even still alive!

Cora walks down the rows. She runs a finger across the spines of all the books on the shelves along the way.

"Nope. Nope. Not that one. Nope. No. No. Nope."

"What are you looking for?" I ask. "Or, *who* are you looking for?"

"No. No. No. Nope." Cora comes back my way, her finger one shelf higher now. She's so into finding a book, she's not even listening to me.

I decide to look around on my own. There's a book about Neil Armstrong. I know he was the first man to walk on the moon. My teacher, Miss Flippo, told my class that. She knows a lot about outer space because she got to go there once. Most people don't believe me when I tell them my teacher used to be an astronaut, but she really, truly was.

On the shelf, there are biographies of presidents. There are biographies of presidents' wives. (They are called First Ladies.) There are biographies of baseball players and swimmers and movie stars. They all look interesting, but what I'm looking for isn't in the *Biographies* section.

I have something else ticking at the back of my brain.

"Cora, I'm going to the computers," I say.

"Nope. No. Not that one," she answers. Her finger is now running along the books four shelves from the floor, and she has to stand on her tiptoes to reach.

Wow, she's really focused on finding that book. I can't imagine who she wants to read about. I head to the computers to do some serious research.

Luckily, Aunt Darian showed Cora and me how to find any library book using

the online search catalog. *Hmmm.* I wonder
if I should go remind Cora about that. No,
when her finger gets tired of running along
the edges of books, she'll use the computer.

In the search box, I type the words: *perfect
pets.* The little circle spins around for a few
seconds and then a long list of books comes
up on the screen. I read some of the titles:
*How to Care for Aquarium Fish, Training Your
New Puppy.*

I don't need to know how to care for or
train a pet if I don't even know
what kind of pet I want.

I decide to change my search words: *choosing a pet. Aha!* Now, that's better.

Beside the computer, there are some scraps of paper and short little pencils. I write down the numbers and letters for the book I want and then I tiptoe over to the children's nonfiction section. The library is open now, and people are coming inside, quietly stomping snow off their boots at the door.

Last week, I heard Mom and Dad talking in the kitchen. I'm pretty sure they didn't know I was there, because they got really quiet when I came into the room, and they started talking about when it might snow. But I know that's not what they were talking about before. They were talking about getting another pet! We've had Sloan for a long time, and he's the best dog ever, but everyone in my family loves animals, and I've been asking for another pet for a long, long time!

If the Watkins family is getting a new pet, I need to research every pet in the world, so we get the best pet ever.

I find the book I'm looking for, *Choosing the Right Pet*, just as Cora comes down the steps with a biography in her hand. She must have run out of "nopes" and found a "yep."

"What did you find?" I ask.

Cora smiles and shows me the cover.

"*King Tut: Decorated Pharaoh*," I read. "Is that who you were looking for?"

"Yep," Cora answers.

"King Tut and Cindy Sparkles are really, really different," I say.

"No, they're not," Cora insists. "King Tut was the first person to wear sequins." She turns some pages in the book until she comes to a photo of tiny, metal sequins. They don't have much shine to them anymore. And they look really old. "See? King Tut sparkled!"

You can't argue with that.

KING TUT

DECORATED PHARAOH
By Lois Bloomberry

Chapter Three

The Lunch Table

The next day, the sun is shining, but Dad was wrong about the snow melting quickly. There is still plenty of it stuck to the grass and trees. The roads are all clear, but I wait until the last minute to get out of my warm pajamas, just in case the robo-call comes.

It doesn't, so I almost miss the bus. Luckily, my bus driver, Mr. McHenry, blows the horn and waits for me to run down the sidewalk in my new, brown snow boots.

Brown is my favorite color because all the best things in the world are brown:

chocolate, mud, earthworms. My hair, and even Miss Flippo's hair.

Miss Flippo is the best teacher ever, and Room 2-C is the best classroom in all of Granite City Elementary School. Cora is in Room 2-C. And Natalie. And Georgia, who moved all the way from Alabama. And Ajay and Tessa. And—

"Lucy Goosey!" I hear Stewart Swinefest's voice as soon as my brown boots step off Bus 21. I decide to ignore him.

"LUCY GOOSEY!" Stewart yells louder, so I turn around.

"What do you want, Stewart?" I ask.

Stewart is laughing, and so is Brody. Brody always laughs when Stewart laughs. "Nothing." Stewart smirks. "Just wanted to see if you knew your name! LUCY GOOSEY!"

I give Stewart a big eye-roll and walk away. Walking away from Stewart Swinefest is *always* a good decision.

Mrs. James, our principal, is standing inside the big front doors.

"Welcome back," she says. "I hope you enjoyed your day off yesterday."

I smile at Mrs. James. I wonder what she does here at school all day long when we have a snow day. Does she just walk around in the halls all by herself? I would ask her, but I'm kind of in a hurry to get to Room 2-C.

Miss Flippo greets everyone with a smile. I put my backpack on the hook below my name and on my way to my seat, I notice Mr. Bones. Mr. Bones is Miss Flippo's favorite student. He never makes a sound. He stays perfectly still.

He's a skeleton.

And today, for the very first time ever, Mr. Bones is wearing a red wool scarf around his neck. No, it's actually around his *clavicle*. We learned that bone just last week when Ming flew off the swing at recess and fractured hers. *Fractured*, Miss Flippo said, means cracked, but not broken. Not only is Mr. Bones wearing a scarf around his clavicle, but he also has a pair of red mittens covering his long, boney hands.

I start to laugh, and Cora says, "Hey, Lucy. What's so funny?"

"Mr.—"

Miss Flippo claps three times, and I know that means to be quiet.

"I'll tell you later," I whisper to Cora.

Miss Flippo tells us about what she's planned for our day.

"We have extra work to do because school was closed yesterday," she says. Everyone groans about the extra work, but Miss Flippo says she'll open up the Science Lab right after lunch if we have a productive morning. *Productive* is what we are when we get a lot done.

At lunch, I decide to take a survey. Miss Flippo takes surveys all the time. Surveys are when you ask the same question to a whole bunch of people and then you study their answers. There are six people at my lunch table: Natalie, Carl, Logan, Cora, Ming, and me. Ming has her right arm in a black sling that is supposed to hold her shoulder still so her clavicle can get better. I guess six is enough for a survey.

"Okay, listen, everyone," I say, "I'm doing research about pets."

Logan says, "I'm allergic to pets."

"You can't be allergic to every kind of pet," Ming insists.

"I am. I'm allergic to their hair."

"Well, insects don't have hair," Carl says, "so you could have a pet beetle. Or a grasshopper."

"Insects are boring." Logan shrugs his shoulders. "I don't think I'm much of a pet person, anyway."

"Well, I am," I reply. "And I think my parents are going to let us get a new pet very soon."

"Oh!" Cora jumps up. She's so excited, she almost tips over her Princess Purple Power lunch box. "Get a rabbit!"

"Rabbits are nice," Ming agrees.

"They're more than nice," Cora says. "They're fuzzy and so soft! And their little noses go—" Cora's nose wiggles up and down really fast. Logan, who was taking a drink of milk through his straw, starts to laugh. I'm sure that milk is going to squirt out of his nose, but he swallows just in time.

Mr. Farmer, our custodian, comes over and asks Cora to please sit back down. I'll bet he's glad Logan didn't snort milk

through his nose. Mr. Farmer has to clean
up *a lot* of spilled milk every day.

By the time the bell rings, I have one vote
for a rabbit, one for a praying mantis (Carl,
of course), one for a clownfish, one for a
Great Dane, and one for no pet at all. I think
I'm going to have to expand my research
beyond my lunch table.

Chapter Four

A Good Name

Back in Room 2-C, Miss Flippo stands in the front of the room and claps us all quiet.

"I promised I would open the Science Lab this afternoon," she says. "While you were at lunch, I prepared the lab with some new specimens for you to observe."

Everyone turns to the back of the room to see what Miss Flippo has put on the lab table, but it's covered with a white cloth.

"Hey!" Stewart Swinefest yells, even though Room 2-C has a rule about using inside voices. "Look at Mr. Bones!"

I guess I was the only one who noticed Mr. Bones standing in the back of the room in his new red scarf and mittens earlier. Now the whole class is giggling and talking, and Miss Flippo has to clap us all quiet again.

"Yes, Stewart." Miss Flippo is smiling. "I've given Mr. Bones some winter accessories to match the snowy weather we had yesterday." Then her smile turns to frown. "I'm sorry I couldn't find a hat to match, though. I think his skull looks a bit chilly, don't you?"

Miss Flippo walks to the back of the room and stands beside the lab table. "Okay, scientists, can anyone guess what our new science unit is about?" she asks as she lifts the white cloth from the lab table.

Since I sit in the front row, I am pretty far from the Science Lab. I stand up to see better. So do Logan, Carl, and Jack. It looks like there are a lot of rocks on the table.

"Rocks?" Heather guesses.

"You're half right, Heather," Miss Flippo explains as she holds up a flat gray stone. "These specimens are interesting because they have something *in* them."

"Diamonds!" Collin guesses.

26

"That's silly," Stewart tells Collin. "Diamonds don't come from rocks!"

Collin scowls. "Yes, they do. My mom says the diamond in her wedding ring came from a diamond mine!"

Stewart opens his mouth to argue with Collin some more, but Miss Flippo jumps in just in time.

"Diamonds are precious gems," she says, "and they do come out of rocks, sometimes deep inside the earth."

Collin nods his head. Now it's Stewart's turn to scowl.

"But I'm sure you won't find any diamonds in the specimens I've brought today," Miss Flippo says. "Diamonds are found mostly in Africa. When it's your turn to come back to the Science Lab, you'll use your eyes and these magnifying glasses to see if you can find any *fossils* hidden in these rocks."

"What are fossils?" Sarah asks.

"Dinosaurs!" It's Collin again. I have never seen him so excited about science.

"That's right. Creatures who walked the earth a very long time ago often left behind fossils."

Miss Flippo returns to the front of the room and turns on her computer. The whiteboard lights up so we can all see what Miss Flippo sees on her screen.

"Fossils are clues," she says. "They give us hints about what might have been living long ago. Let's take a look at some famous fossils."

Miss Flippo shows us all kinds of rocks with prints in them. Some look like bugs. Others look like leaves. One looks like a turtle.

"This one is very famous," Miss Flippo says. "What do you think it is?"

We all stare at the picture on the whiteboard.

Gavin raises his hand. "It looks like a bird."

"Why do you say that, Gavin?" Miss Flippo asks.

"Because it has wings," he says.

"And a beak," Ajay adds.

"Anyone else?" Miss Flippo asks. Annalisa raises her hand. "Annalisa?"

"It could be a small dinosaur . . . " she says.

"And why do you think that?"

"It has long legs." Annalisa's head is turned sideways. "I *think* those are legs."

"Very good, my scientists," Miss Flippo says. "This is actually *Archaeopteryx*. And you're all correct. It is believed to be both a bird and dinosaur. It was discovered more than 150 years ago, but it lived about 150 *million* years ago."

All of Room 2-C goes *Whoa!* at the same time.

"Scientists who studied this fossil believe that creatures like this dinosaur-bird were the ancestors of the birds we see flying around our backyards today."

I look at the whiteboard closely. I can see how that could happen.

The next picture is definitely not a dinosaur. It looks like Mr. Bones, but with some bones missing.

"That's a person," Jack says quietly.

"Yes, they believe it was an early human," Miss Flippo agrees. "Still very different from you and me, but when scientists look at fossils like this and then compare them to other fossils, they can learn how humans have changed over time."

I notice Miss Flippo is smiling at me. I don't know why, so I just smile right back.

"This famous fossil has a name," Miss Flippo tells us. "They call her Lucy."

Everyone laughs and looks right at me, but I'm not embarrassed. I think it's cool to share a name with a famous fossil.

Later, while I'm waiting for my turn at the lab table, I hear Stewart Swinefest whispering to Collin and Brody, "Lucy's not a goosey! She's a fossil!"

Who invited Stewart to second grade, anyway? I'd sure like to know.

Chapter Five

Family Meeting

At home, we have a family meeting while we eat dinner. Dad made his most wonderful chili soup, and Thomas is piling his bowl high with a million tiny crackers.

"I call the Watkins family meeting to order," Mom says. "Roll call, please, Lucy."

"Dad?" I say.

"Present." Dad says.

"Mom?" I say.

"Here," she answers.

"Lucy?" I ask. "Here," I answer.

"Thomas?" I say.

"Mmmwwhhhmm," he answers. Too many crackers. Way too many crackers.

"Very well, then," Dad says. "What matter of business should the Watkins family discuss first?"

"I have something!" I say, although I can't quite decide if I want to talk about a new pet or a really old fossil named Lucy.

"Go ahead, Lucy," says Mom.

I choose the new pet topic. "Since we're getting another pet soon, I have been doing some research."

Mom looks at Dad.

Dad looks at Mom.

Thomas chews like crazy and then swallows hard. "We're getting *another* dog? Really?"

"Slow down, Thomas," I say. "Nobody said anything about getting a second dog."

"Nobody said anything about a second pet, either," Dad said. "At least not to you, Lucy."

Oops. I kind of forgot that I wasn't exactly part of the conversation I heard my parents having in the kitchen.

"Lucy," Mom asks, "have you been eavesdropping?"

"Well, not on purpose," I say. "You were talking and I started listening before I was supposed to."

"Since Lucy brought up the subject, I say we talk about it," Dad says.

"I want another dog!" Thomas sounds like his mind is already made up.

"We already know that a dog is a good pet," Dad agrees.

"But dogs are a lot of work," Mom says. "A second dog would have to be fed, groomed, and walked just like Sloan. A cat might be less time-consuming."

"Dogs? Cats? Where's your imagination, people?" I roll my eyes. Dogs and cats are so—*ordinary*.

"What would you suggest, Lucy?" Mom asks.

"I don't know. I'm not finished with my research yet."

"Well, that's probably a good thing," Dad says, "because we're not quite ready to commit to adding a second pet to this household. You do your research, Lucy, and we'll talk about it again later."

"Sounds like a good plan," Mom agrees.

"I'm fine with that," I say.

"If we can't get another dog, then I want a dinosaur." Thomas says. He's totally serious.

Chapter Six

Survey

When I wake up the next morning, every bit of the snow is gone.

"That's an early season snowfall for you," Dad says. "Easy come, easy go."

I like the snow, but I'm kind of happy it melted. Miss Flippo told us we could look for our own fossils and bring them in to share with the class. It would be pretty hard to hunt for fossils under the snow.

Bus 21 pulls up in front of our school and I wave goodbye to Mr. McHenry. I can see Cora standing on the sidewalk waiting for me. She's wearing striped leggings with a pink and purple dress under her winter coat.

"Can you believe the snow is gone?" she asks. "My mom says we won't even need our heavy coats later today!"

"That's good," I say. "Let's go fossil hunting after school."

Cora and I agree to meet in my lab later. The science lab in my backyard used to be a playhouse, but when school started this year, I decided that research and observation are way more important for a second grader than playing *house*.

Last night after supper, I asked to use Mom's computer. I wanted to make a bigger survey, since my survey at lunch didn't go so well. I came up with even more questions, and we used her printer and made twenty copies for the twenty kids in Room 2-C.

As soon as I walk through the door, I tell Miss Flippo about my survey.

"Hold onto those until after the morning announcements, Lucy," she tells me. I wonder what she has planned, but right after the announcements are over, she calls me to the front of the room.

"Class, Lucy is gathering information. Another word for information is *data*. Lucy is going to pass out a survey. There are four questions to answer."

Miss Flippo keeps talking while I walk down each row, handing out my surveys.

"I'd like you to think about each question, and then fill it out. When you've completed the survey, place it in the basket on my desk.

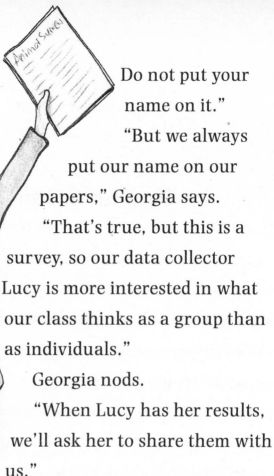

Do not put your
name on it."

"But we always
put our name on our
papers," Georgia says.

"That's true, but this is a
survey, so our data collector
Lucy is more interested in what
our class thinks as a group than
as individuals."

Georgia nods.

"When Lucy has her results,
we'll ask her to share them with
us."

Wow. I had no idea my survey
would be such a big deal!

Chapter Seven

Fossil Failure

Bus 21 drops me off at my house after school. In my backpack, I have all the surveys that were in Miss Flippo's tray at the end of the day. A wonderful smell is coming from the kitchen, so I go check it out.

"Hi, Lucy," Dad says. "How was school?"

"Good," I say. "What are you making?"

"Cookies. There's no snow to scrape today, and there won't be any grass to mow for a long time so I decided to make a treat," Dad says. "Want one?"

Cinnamon snickerdoodles! My favorite! "Can I take two? One for me and one for Cora?"

"Of course," says Dad, "but you know you can't eat them in the library."

"Oh, I know. We're going to the park today."

There are three places in Granite City I'm allowed to go without my parents: Cora's house, the library, and the park. Cora's, because it's only three blocks and I don't have to cross a road to get there; the library, because Aunt Darian is the librarian and it's right behind Cora's house; and the park, because it's pretty much in my backyard.

I change into my brown snow boots while Dad wraps up two warm cookies. I don't really need to wear snow boots now that the snow is gone, but the park might be muddy.

"Thanks, Dad!" I yell on my way out to my lab. "Be back before supper!"

Dad reminds me that it gets dark earlier than it used to, so I'll need to be back sooner.

In the backyard, I take a look at my old playhouse/new science lab. I haven't been inside it for a few days, so I duck through the door to check things out. All my specimens from the fall are still sitting on the table. My lab notebook is kind of damp and the pages look crinkly. I guess I'll have to take it inside before it snows again.

Through the window, I can see Cora coming down the sidewalk.

"Good afternoon, Princess Lucy," she bows at the door.

Ugh. I don't really like Cora's princess
games. "I regret to inform you that Princess
Lucy has been eaten by a dragon," I say.

Cora looks shocked. "How awful! So, who
are you then?"

"The dragon!" I yell, running toward
Cora, pretending to breathe fire at her.

Cora screams and laughs, and we both
run through my backyard and into the

Granite City Park. The park was the reason my parents bought our house. My mom always says that she liked the house just fine, but after she saw the park, she loved it. "It's like having our very own nature preserve!" she tells people.

We stop running near the jungle gym. "Where should we start looking for fossils?" Cora asks.

"Well, I guess we go wherever there are rocks," I say.

Standing at the jungle gym, all I can see is grass. Lots and lots of grass.

"There are rocks in the parking lot," Cora suggests.

I'm not sure that parking lot rocks are the kind of rocks that have fossils in them, but they are the only rocks I can see. We walk over to the gravel parking lot. The little bits of gray gravel all look the same, kind of dusty white with jagged edges.

"Okay," Cora says. "I hope we find dinosaur bones!"

"That would be exciting." I am just hoping we find the fossil of a small bug or something interesting like that.

We walk bent over and stare at the ground. We don't say a word for a long time.

"Do you see anything interesting?" I ask. I pick up a small stone, but it is just like all the others.

"Some of the rocks sparkle a little," Cora says. "Any fossils over there?"

"Nope," I say. I stand up straight. Bending over for so long makes my back hurt.

Cora stands up, too. "I think it's getting dark," she says, looking up at the sky.

It was cloudy all afternoon, so we didn't get to see the sun setting. Cora's right about it getting dark, so we walk kind of fast across the grass and into my backyard.

"Well, that wasn't very exciting," I say.

Cora laughs. "But the two princesses did get back to the castle before dark!"

"Correction," I say. "One princess and one"—I run toward Cora, chasing her down the sidewalk toward her house. I can hear her giggling all the way—"dragon!"

Chapter Eight

Survey Says . . .

After supper, I am excited to see what my classmates wrote on my surveys. Mom is, too. We lay the completed sheets out on the kitchen table.

"Tally time!" Mom says. "Lucy, you take notes while I read the responses. Ready?"

"Ready!" I say. "Question one: Do you have a pet at your house?"

I write the words YES and NO at the top of my paper. I make a short little line every time Mom reads YES or NO.

"Now, count them," Mom says. I count 14 YESes and 3 NOs.

"Okay, then," says Mom, "let's move on to question two."

"Wait," I say. Something isn't right. I scribble a little math problem on the paper. Fourteen plus three equals—seventeen. "Mom! There are only seventeen answers. And there are twenty kids in Room 2-C."

"Well, let's see," says Mom. "Did you fill out a survey?"

"Oh! Nope, I didn't."

"So, you should have 19 surveys. But it looks like only 17 people turned theirs in." Mom has her thinking face on. "Eighty-nine percent of your class responded. That's very good, actually."

Good? I don't think that sounds very good. I'm kind of grouchy that two of my classmates didn't give me their answers. I'll bet it was Stewart and Brody. Or maybe Logan, since he said at lunch that he wasn't much of a pet person.

"Let's keep going. Question two," Mom says. "'If you have a pet, what kind do you have?' Okay, you'll have to do more writing on this one."

Mom reads the words *cat* and *dog* a lot. She says *goldfish* and *tropical fish* and *cockatiel*, which I don't know how to spell. Once she says *ferret* and *hermit crab* and *tarantula*. When she gets done, I count twenty-three pets.

"Wow! I didn't think there would be so many!" I say.

"I agree," says Mom. "A lot of families have more than one pet!"

I count totals for each animal. Then we move on to question three.

"If you could have any pet at all, what pet would you choose?" Mom reads. "Ready?"

"Go," I say.

I write down *rabbit* and *tiger cub* and *corn snake*. I write down *kitten* and *talking parrot* and lots of other pets my classmates in Room 2-C wish they could have.

"Someone wrote *Madagascar hissing cockroach*," Mom says, making an awful face.

"That has to be Carl," I say. "Only Carl loves insects *that* much."

I count everything up and write all the totals on a clean piece of paper. Then I make a graph that shows all the animals and the number of people who like them. That's what I'll share with Room 2-C tomorrow. Now I know what pets my classmates have or want to have.

Problem is, I still have no clue what pet *I* want.

Chapter Nine

The Data, Please

At school, I can't wait to share my survey results. Miss Flippo saves time right after recess.

"Scientists, let's listen to Lucy," she says. "Lucy, tell us what your data shows, please."

I take my paper to the front of the room, and Miss Flippo gives me her tall stool to sit on.

"My data shows that the students in Room 2-C have a total of twenty-three pets. The most popular pet is dogs. There are twelve dogs. The second most popular pet is cats. There are six cats. The most unusual pet is a tarantula."

"Oh, that is a wonderful pet," Miss Flippo exclaims. "Who has a tarantula?"

I wait for someone to raise their hand. I'm sure it will be Eddie or Carl or maybe Jack. So I'm surprised when I see Bridget raises her hand instead.

"We got him when we lived New York City," she says. "Our apartment manager didn't allow dogs."

"What else, Lucy?" Miss Flippo asks.

"Well, a lot of kids want pets. Eight kids want dogs. Somebody wants a hissing cockroach."

58

Lots of kids in the room laugh or make grossed out noises. I look at Carl. He's grinning.

"Are you the cockroach fan, Carl?" Miss Flippo smiles at him.

"Only if it's a Madagascar hissing cockroach," he says. "Those are the best."

"All right, then. We've got some insects, arachnids, and mammals on our list," Miss Flippo says. "Any reptiles?"

"Someone wants a leopard gecko," I tell her.

"Reptiles are the closest living relatives to the dinosaurs of long ago," Miss Flippo tells us. "And speaking of dinosaurs, we'll be continuing our discussion about fossils right after noon recess. But first, Lucy, was your survey helpful? Did you figure out what kind of pet you and your family might get?"

"At first, I didn't think so." I can't help

but smile really big. "But just now, I think I figured it out!"

Miss Flippo and Room 2-C have given me a great idea.

Cora comes home with me every Tuesday and stays for dinner, because that's the night the library is open late. Aunt Darian swings by when the library closes and gets Cora.

Since Dad has a meeting tonight and he can't cook like usual, Mom brings home pizza for dinner. Sometimes, people think it's funny that my dad does all the cooking, but I'm glad he does. Mom doesn't even like to cook!

Thomas roars into the room with a T. rex in his hand.

"Dinos love pizza!" he shouts, climbing into a chair and setting the T. rex next to the pizza box.

"Dig in," Mom says. "Pizza's getting cold."

"Speaking of digging," I say, "where are we ever going to find fossils? Our trip to the park was a big failure."

"Well, it sounds like you just answered your own question," Mom says in her professor voice. "Most fossils are hidden deep in the ground until the earth gets disturbed for some reason."

"So we need to go *digging*?" Cora asks.

Why didn't I think of that? We only looked at rocks *on top* of the ground at the park. But wouldn't the park manager be unhappy if we went digging in the city park? Suddenly, I have an idea.

"Maybe we need to go someplace where the ground has already been dug up!"

Cora's eyes light up, and we both say it. "The stone quarry!"

Mom smiles. "You're on the right track, but there are several problems."

Cora and I groan at the same time.

"Well, beside that fact that stone quarries are dangerous places for two young scientists to be roaming around, I'm afraid you're not going to find many, if any, fossils at the Granite City Quarry."

"Why?" I ask.

"Because our stone quarry is filled with granite," Mom says. "That's why our town is called Granite City."

"But why can't we find fossils in granite?" I want to know.

Mom explains. "Because there are many kinds of rock. Some rocks are harder—like granite—and some are softer. Granite is igneous rock, the marble on the bathroom counter is metamorphic rock, and most fossils are found in softer, sedimentary rock."

"Well, where are we going to find *that* kind of rock?" Cora asks.

Mom thinks for a minute. "I know."

She gets up from the table and pulls her phone out of her purse. She punches a few buttons and puts it to her ear. Cora and I both reach for another piece of pizza.

"Who is she calling?" Cora giggles.

"I have no idea," I say. My mom knows a lot of people.

After a short conversation and a lot of "okay" and "all right, then" and "thank you," Mom hangs up the phone.

"It's all settled! We're going fossil hunting on the banks of the Nine-Mile Creek this Saturday!"

"I'm going, too!" says the T. rex in front of Thomas's face.

Not if I have anything to say about it.

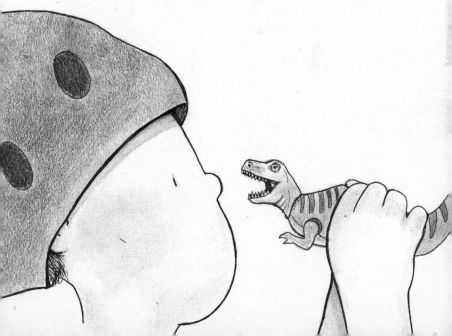

Chapter Ten

Dig, Dip, Look, *Plunk*!

On Saturday morning, the sun is shining brightly, and I'm awake and ready to go before Mom is even out of her fuzzy robe and slippers.

"It's going to be a nice late-autumn day," Mom says, finishing her coffee. "I'll be ready in a jiffy!"

Thomas tromps down the stairs in his brachiosaurus pajamas. He's still yawning and his hair looks like a dinosaur licked his head while he was asleep.

"Where are you going?" Thomas yawns.

"Fossil hunting," I tell him. "With Cora."

"I'm going with you!" Suddenly, Thomas is wide awake. "I can be ready in a jippy, too!"

"Mom!" I protest. "Thomas isn't really going with us, is he?"

"Sorry, Lucy," Mom says. "Your dad's using big leaf-blowing equipment this morning, and there's no safe place for Thomas when Dad's working."

"Ugh. Well, he better stay out of the way," I moan.

"Look at it this way, Lucy." Mom smiles. "At least he can't scare the fossils away."

I'm not so sure about that.

The Nine-Mile Creek is really just a stream that runs through town, out across Farmer

Dan's pasture, through the woods and then under the highway. After that, I don't know where the Nine-Mile goes.

Last summer, Mom and Thomas watched a big digger scrape out the banks of the creek. Thomas was amazed at how the big machine could chomp into the dirt and pull the edges of the creek away.

We start out walking along the high bank, but pretty soon I figure out that the water's only up to my ankles, so I start sloshing right down the middle of the creek bed. Cora tiptoes down the muddy bank to join me.

"I was hoping I wouldn't get my purple boots dirty," she fusses.

"You won't if you walk in the creek," I say.

"Keep your eyes on the banks for evidence of life from the Paleozoic Era," Mom says.

"Pay-lee-o what?" Cora asks.

"Many fossils found in this area are from a time called the Paleozoic Era," Mom explains. "That was around 300 to 500 million years ago."

"Whoa! I want to find a Paleozoic fossil!" I say.

"I found one!" Thomas shouts. He's holding an ordinary rock from the creek.

"Mom," I beg. "Please tell Thomas to stay out of the way."

"He'll stay right beside me," she promises. "You two go on ahead."

"Let's go!" I say, and Cora and I run through the shallow water, making big splashes with our boots.

Mom was right. The rain has washed away the dirt from the sides that were scraped away last summer, and rocks of all sizes are poking out of the creek bank. We stop to inspect every last pebble.

Before long, I've got a system. Dig out the rock with my fingers, dip it in water to clean it off, turn it over to look for fossils, and then chuck it over my shoulder into the creek if I don't see anything interesting. The bigger ones land with a *plunk*!

On we go. Dig, dip, look, *plunk*! Dig, dip, look, *plunk*!

Cora's the first to find a fossil treasure.

"Look at this!" she cries after a dip.

I stop digging and go to see what she's discovered. Mom catches up and looks over our shoulders.

"See these lines?" Cora squeals. "I think it's a plant!"

Sure enough, the small rock she's holding has a row of lines going one direction and a row of lines going the other direction.

"Like a fern," Mom agrees.

"Oooh! I found a fossil! I found a fossil!"
Cora is jumping up and down. Muddy water
splashes everywhere and she doesn't even
care!

Now, I'm really determined to find
something. I start digging, dipping, looking,
and plunking faster. I try not to skip a single
rock. I don't want the one I
skip to be the one that has
best fossil ever in it.

Mom finds something
that looks like a tiny worm
fossil, but she says she
can't be sure. We add it
to the plastic bag that's
holding Cora's fern
fossil for safe-keeping.
And then, I see it.

It looks like a
branch sticking

out of the mud. I walk over to inspect it, and I can see it isn't made of wood. It's hard as a rock.

I start to do my dig, dip, look thing, but all I can do is dig. Dig. Dig more.

"Hey, Mom!"

Cora and Mom help me dig the rock out of the mud. It's as long as my arm and it's broken off on both ends. I dip it in the water to clean it off, and then we all just stare at it for a minute.

"Plunk it." Cora sighs. "I don't see any fossils on it."

Mom looks at me. Her eyes are all excited, and she laughs. "I don't think we want to plunk this, Cora. You can't see any fossils on it, because—I think—the whole thing is a fossil."

I stare at the find I'm holding. "Is it a bone?"

"Maybe," Mom says. "I honestly don't know, but I think it's worth showing to someone."

"It's a T. rex bone," Thomas says with confidence.

"How do you know?" Cora asks.

Thomas shrugs. "I just know."

"Miss Flippo will know," I say.

My long bone-fossil-thing is too big to fit in the little plastic bag, so I carry it under my arm as we walk back toward the car along the other side of the creek.

Along the way, we find two more rocks that look like snails might have left behind fossil clues for us. Mom adds those to the bag, and by the time we get back to where we started, we're wet, muddy, and very curious.

I can't wait to hear what Room 2-C will say about our fossil-hunting finds!

Chapter Eleven

A Colossal Fossil Fib

On Monday, I don't ride the bus to school, because Mr. McHenry might not like it if I bring a long chunk of rock on the bus. Instead, Dad drops me off. We get there early because Dad's always early for everything.

"It's okay," I tell Dad. "I can stop by the school library and see if Mrs. Alvarez needs any help."

I take my fossil to Room 2-C. It's weird in there with the lights out. I tiptoe past Mr. Bones.

"Don't mind me, Mr. B.," I say. He doesn't

move a muscle. Of course, he doesn't have any muscles to move.

After I hang up my coat and backpack, I put all my specimens on the counter in the Science Lab. I can't wait for Miss Flippo to see the big one we found at the creek on Saturday.

The lights are on in the library, so I offer to help Mrs. Alvarez put books back on the shelves. She's usually very picky about books being in the right place, but she knows that my Aunt Darian works at the public library, so she trusts Cora and me.

We talk about how November in Granite City can be cold and snowy like the other day, or warm and sunny like today is supposed to be. There's always something wonderful about Mrs. Alvarez's library. Everything is in order and I like the way the books smell.

Soon, I hear the screech of bus brakes and see a hundred kids walking into school.

"Gotta go meet my cousin Cora," I say, darting out into the hallway. It's hard to walk toward the front doors with everyone else on their way to their classrooms. But I want to be right inside when Cora gets off her bus so that we can tell Miss Flippo about our fossil adventures together.

When Cora's bus pulls up, lots of kids get off, but not one with a pink tutu or purple sparkly tights. When her bus pulls away, I give up and head to Room 2-C. The room is buzzing with kids, taking off coats and talking to each other.

I stop dead in my tracks, when I see who Miss Flippo is talking to.

Stewart Swinefest is holding *my* newly-found fossil.

Miss Flippo has an enormous smile on her face as she listens to Stewart.

"I found it yesterday," I hear him say. "Right in my backyard!"

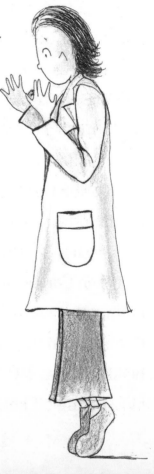

Chapter Twelve

Staying on the Handle

How dare Stewart Swinefest tell a lie like that!

I march right up to Miss Flippo's desk.

"Lucy, you'll be excited to see what Stewart found," she says.

Stewart grins.

"He didn't find it," I tell her. I stay calm. Dad would tell me that nothing good comes from "flying off the handle." When he says that, I imagine a witch on her broom on a really windy day working hard just to stay seated on her broom handle.

"He didn't?" Miss Flippo asks.

Before I can explain, Stewart jumps in. "Yes, I did. In my yard. Yesterday."

Just to make himself sound more believable, he adds, "I did." I start to get worried because Stewart looks really sincere.

Miss Flippo looks at me.

"I found it. Saturday. I went walking on the Nine-Mile Creek."

Stewart holds the long fossil rock even tighter. I'm glad it's too hard to break, the way he's squeezing.

"Stewart," Miss Flippo says. "Tell me the truth."

But Stewart Swinefest stands his ground. "I did. I told you. I found it in my backyard yesterday."

I feel myself flying off the handle. How could he? How could just lie like that?

"He's lying," I say. "I was here early and I put it in the Science Lab, and he took it!"

Miss Flippo's forehead is all wrinkled up. "This is very concerning," she says. "Someone is not telling the truth, and you both know that honesty is something I expect, always."

Stewart nods, and I feel tears coming to my eyes. Then, it hits me. I spin around.

"Cora!" I call out. I'm not using my quiet voice, but I don't care. Where is Cora? She was there with me on Saturday. She'll tell Miss Flippo.

"Cora!"

"Lucy," Miss Flippo says. "Cora's mother called her in sick today. Cora's not here."

Cora's sick? Ugh. Now there's no one who can prove I'm telling the truth.

The bell rings, but no one moves. Everyone is waiting to see how Miss Flippo's going resolve this big problem. *I'm* waiting to see how Miss Flippo's going to resolve this big problem!

Finally, she reaches out and takes the fossil—*my* fossil—from Stewart's hands. "I'll tell you what," she says. "I'm going to keep this for a little while, until we can solve the issue of who found it and who owns it now. You may both sit down."

Stewart runs to his desk. I walk to mine. It's going to be a long Monday without Cora.

After dinner, Mom calls Aunt Darian. Cora's got strep throat, and she'll miss at least two more days of school. Mom tells Aunt Darian to call if they need anything, then she hangs up the phone.

"This is awful!" I say.

"Well, strep throat is no fun, but Cora will get better, Lucy," Mom says.

I feel bad for Cora, but that's not what's got me so upset. I pace around the room. "You don't understand, Mom! Stewart stole my fossil, and I'm trying really hard not to fall off my broom!"

Mom looks confused. "You're right on one thing, Lucy. I *don't* understand what you're talking about."

I tell her everything about getting to school early and putting the fossil on the specimen counter. I tell her about Stewart lying, and how I was counting on Cora to tell Miss Flippo the truth.

"Now how will I prove it's mine?" I ask. "You have to write a note, Mom. Please tell Miss Flippo about how we found the fossil."

Mom thinks for a long time before she answers. "Of course I'll let Miss Flippo know about how we found the fossil at the Nine-Mile Creek."

Whew! I knew I could count on Mom to save the day.

"*But*, let's give Stewart a day to think about his lie. I have a hunch he'll do the right thing if he's given a little time."

I think that's the most ridiculous idea I've ever heard. But I guess it won't hurt to give Stewart a chance to be honest.

"Okay," I agree.

Mom smiles. "There's still something I don't understand, though. What's this about staying on your broom?"

"Oh," I say. "You know, I've been trying not to fly off the handle. I'm trying to stay on my broom like a witch in a windstorm."

Mom laughs out loud. "Well, you're using that phrase the right way, Lucy, but I don't think that it came from flying on a broom."

"It didn't?" I ask. "Where did it come from?"

"Do a little research," Mom says. "See if you can find out."

Great. More homework!

Chapter Thirteen

Truth Be Told

On Tuesday morning, the breakfast talk is all about pets again. It seems Thomas has been doing some research of his own.

"We're getting a dinosaur," he says. "I want a stegosaurus."

"Dinosaurs are huge!" I say.

"Dinosaurs are extinct," Dad adds.

"Yeah, that's a problem, too," I agree.

But Thomas won't back down. "We can buy air freshener if it stinks!"

"*Extinct*," I tell Thomas. "Extinct means there aren't any more dinosaurs."

Thomas isn't happy about this news. He starts to pout and pushes his peanut butter toast away.

"Don't worry," I say. "I've figured out the perfect pet for our family."

Dad looks surprised. "Have you?"

"Yep," I say. "And when the time is right, I'll let you all know."

At school, I speed-walk to Room 2-C. I about have a heart attack when I see that my very

special fossil is not on the counter in the Science Lab. I take a peek at Miss Flippo's desk, but just a quick one. Teachers are pretty picky about students nosing around their desks. Still, a rock that size should be easy to spot, and I don't see it anywhere.

"Have you seen Miss Flippo?" I ask Ming, who is hanging up her coat.

"No, but her sweater is on the back of her chair, so I know she's here." I look at Miss Flippo's chair. Ming's right. She's a good observer.

Pretty soon, Miss Flippo comes in the room, and she looks even more excited about being at school than usual, and Miss Flippo is one of the most excited people I know. She claps and everyone stops what they're doing.

"Room 2-C! Let's hurry to our seats. I have something to share before

Mrs. James comes on with the morning announcements!"

Stewart walks in the room just as everyone is scurrying to sit down.

"Whoa, what's going on?" he asks.

"Have a seat, Stewart." Miss Flippo beams. "You're going to be very interested in what I have to say."

"Is it about my fossil?" Stewart asks.

"*My* fossil," I say.

"*My* . . ." Stewart starts to argue, but Miss Flippo shushes him.

When everyone is sitting, Miss Flippo says, "I have some very interesting news about the fossil that *someone* found over the weekend."

91

Room 2-C is very quiet.

"Yesterday, after school, I took the fossil to one of the high school science teachers. He was so amazed by what he saw, that he immediately took it to the university. There, one of the paleontology professors examined it."

"Wow!"

"Whoa!"

Miss Flippo continues, "He believes it could be a part of a wooly mammoth's tusk!"

Room 2-C explodes with chatter until Miss Flippo gets our attention again.

"This is a very important and exciting discovery," she says. "The professor is sending it off to be studied, and we'll know more in about a week. In the meantime, he wants to visit the place where the fossil was found."

All eyes turn to Stewart Swinefest, who isn't celebrating. Instead, he's shrinking. Lower and lower into his seat he slides.

"Stewart?" Miss Flippo asks. "Would you be able to show the professor the exact spot that you found the fossil?"

Stewart looks greener than he did the day he ate too many apples on the field trip to the orchard.

"Yes," he says quietly.

Yes? Is he really going to keep on lying?

Stewart slinks out of his seat and walks

over to the specimen counter. "Right here," he barely whispers. "I'm sorry. I lied. I didn't find it in my backyard. I found it sitting here before school."

Miss Flippo tells Stewart she's pleased he has decided to tell the truth, but she'd like to talk to him at recess.

"So, then," she says. "Lucy, would *you* be able show the professor exactly where you found the fossil?"

I sit up straight and tall. "You bet!"

Chapter 14

A Mammoth Decision

In the backyard after school, I find Dad chopping up a small limb that fell from one of our trees.

"Glad this missed your playhouse, Lucy," Dad says as his ax hits the branch and snaps it two.

"My lab, Dad!" I correct him. "It's my science lab."

"Oh, of course. I forgot," Dad says. "Stand back, you never know when an ax head could fly off its handle."

Oh, my goodness! Is that really why people say "fly off the handle"? I can't wait to tell Mom that I figured it out. Well, kind of. I didn't really have to do any research.

I tell Dad all about Miss Flippo and the professor and the fossil and Stewart's confession.

"Well, what do you know? A wooly mammoth! Don't tell Thomas, or that'll be the next animal he decides he wants as a pet!"

"Speaking of pets, do you think we can go to the pet store this weekend?"

"Are we looking or buying?" he asks.

"I guess that will be up to you!"

On Friday, Cora is back at school. She brings the fern-like fossil she found at the Nine-Mile Creek. Miss Flippo puts it in the Science Lab for the whole class to observe with magnifying glasses.

"You missed all the excitement," I tell Cora while we're in line to sharpen our pencils.

"Well, not *all* the excitement," Miss Flippo says. I didn't even know she was behind me! "I have some news from the university."

Miss Flippo winks, and I know the news must be good.

When Mrs. James has finished saying the announcements over the loud speaker, Miss Flippo calls us to our morning meeting.

"The paleontologist from the university called with some information about Lucy's fossil."

I sit up on my knees. The whole room is quiet. It's like waiting for a big award to be announced.

"Early testing shows the fossil is most likely from the Ice Age, and almost certainly a part of a wooly mammoth's tusk!" she says, smiling.

"Yippee!" Tessa cries, and everyone claps.

"Lucy, this is very special," Miss Flippo says. "What you found is evidence that can be studied. It could provide important clues to what Granite City was like long before there were people and houses and schools here."

I can't believe it. We were just walking in an ordinary creek in an ordinary field and we found something really important.

When we pull into the driveway on Saturday evening, it's already dark.

"Winter's just around the corner," Dad says, looking at the clear sky full of stars.

"I hope Thomas is still awake," I say as the box on my lap jiggles a little.

"Oh, I'm sure he couldn't possibly sleep until he sees if we brought something home," Dad assures me.

I'm so excited about our new pet, I can hardly stand it. The box feels heavier than I expected it would, and when *it* moves around, the box is unsteady in my hands. Dad holds the door for me, and before I can even get into the living room, Thomas is there in his brachiosaurus pajamas.

When he sees the box, my brother starts to pout. "That box is too small for a dinosaur! You got a guinea pig, didn't you? I don't want a guinea pig. I want a dinosaur."

Mom comes in the room and smiles. "Ah, I see your trip to the pet store was a success!"

We set the box on the kitchen table, and Thomas climbs up on a chair.

"Thomas, you know dinosaurs are extinct," I say. "We couldn't get a dinosaur, but we got the next best thing."

I open the box carefully, and the Bearded Dragon inside looks up at us, showing off his scaly skin and spikey neck. He blinks and takes a few steps, moving his long, lizard tail back and forth.

"You *did* get a dinosaur!" Thomas squeals.

"It's a Bearded Dragon," I say. "And you have to be calm and quiet so that you don't scare it."

"Okay," Thomas whispers. "I will be very quiet." He stares at our newest pet and grins. "I don't want to scare it."

"So," I ask Thomas, "do you like him?"

"Yes!" he cries. "If we can't have a dinosaur, a dragon is perfect! Except—"

"Except, what?"

Thomas shakes his head. "We're going to have to keep it away from Cora."

"Cora? Why?" I ask.

"Because princesses never get along with dragons!"

About the Author

Michelle Houts is the award-winning author of several books for young readers. She lives on a farm with a farmer, some cattle, goats, pigs, and a Great Pyrenees named Hercules. She writes in a restored one-room schoolhouse. As a second-grader, Michelle begged her parents for a chemistry kit but wasn't quite sure what to do when she actually got it. Lucy's Lab allows her to be the scientist she always wanted to be.

About the Illustrator

Elizabeth Zechel is an illustrator and author of the children's book *Is There a Mouse in the Baby's Room?* Her illustrations appear in books such as *Wordsbirds* by Liesl Schillinger, *The Little General and the Giant Snowflake* by Matthea Harvey, and cookbooks such as *Bubby's Homemade Pies* by Jen Bervin and Ron Silver, as well as a variety of magazine and literary journals. She lives in Brooklyn, NY where she teaches kindergarten.